The Way We Should Have Been

Dedication:
My Love

TheWayWeShouldHaveBeen

The Way We Should Have Been

1st Journey:

Longing for My Love

The Way We Should Have Been

I want what we never had so badly. I cannot invest my time in someone else, knowing it will never be as pure and potent as we should have been. You start to fear rejection when your heart has been rejected often. Even when the thing you want most in life is within your grasp, you dismiss it before it can refuse you. That is a lonely life, so you seek to fill that void with whatever is available and safe. The only problem is that it's not what you want; therefore, you cannot give it your full attention because your heart is still holding on to what may be. Even after all of this time.....maybe.

TheWayWeShouldHaveBeen

The Way We Should Have Been

I think about what You may be thinking about. Do You think about me sometimes? Am I ever the forefront thought in Your mind? Do You pick up the phone and contemplate dialing my number but do not have a reason for calling other than to hear my voice and, therefore, change Your mind? Do You care so much not to bother or interfere in my day-to-day life that you forego trying to call or text for fear that I would be too busy to talk? Cause that's what I do.

TheWayWeShouldHaveBeen

The Way We Should Have Been

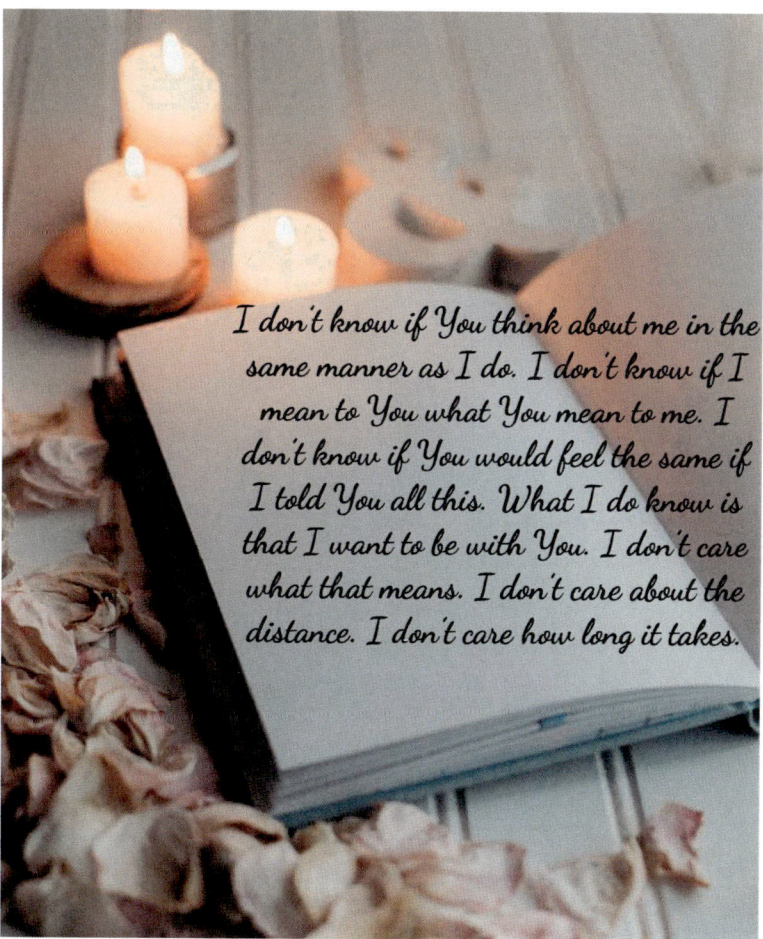

I don't know if You think about me in the same manner as I do. I don't know if I mean to You what You mean to me. I don't know if You would feel the same if I told You all this. What I do know is that I want to be with You. I don't care what that means. I don't care about the distance. I don't care how long it takes.

TheWayWeShouldHaveBeen

The Way We Should Have Been

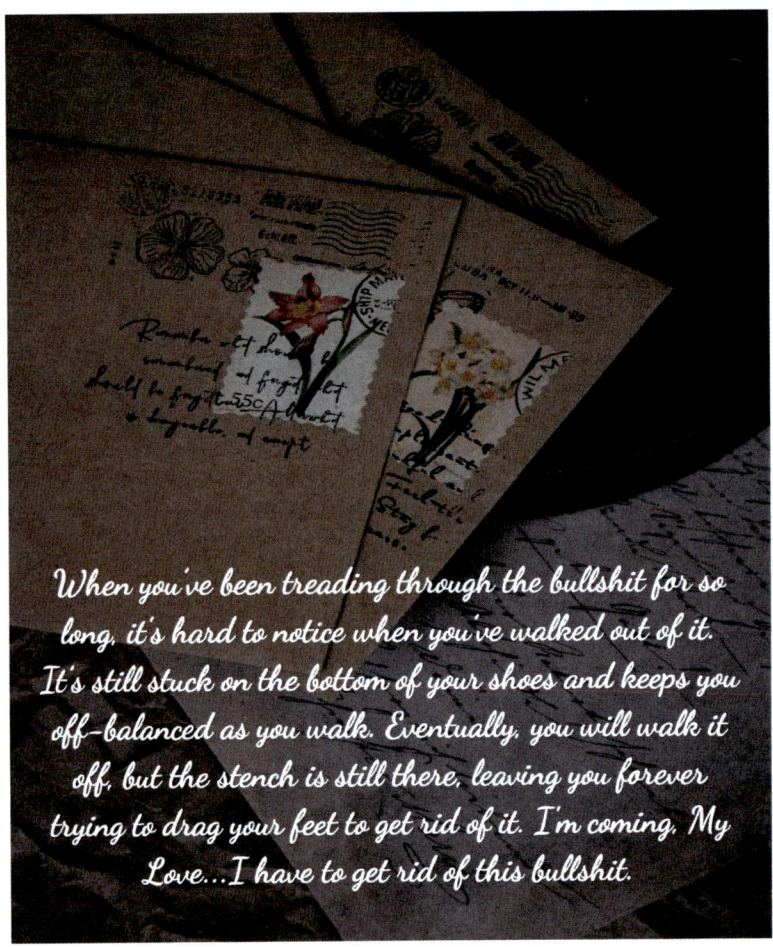

When you've been treading through the bullshit for so long, it's hard to notice when you've walked out of it. It's still stuck on the bottom of your shoes and keeps you off-balanced as you walk. Eventually, you will walk it off, but the stench is still there, leaving you forever trying to drag your feet to get rid of it. I'm coming, My Love...I have to get rid of this bullshit.

The Way We Should Have Been

People change after they've been through a powerfully emotional ordeal. Whether good or bad. I've changed to become a better version of myself for You. You deserve nothing less.

TheWayWeShouldHaveBeen

The Way We Should Have Been

People may believe that the only way to Love someone is to know them inside and out, which can only come after years of knowledge. This is just not true. I have Loved You from the 1st interaction with You. I Love every conversation with You. I Love watching You interact with other people. I Love watching You grow as a person over the years and seeing Your impact on my life. My inner peace Loves Your inner peace, which happened from the beginning.

TheWayWeShouldHaveBeen

The Way We Should Have Been

Maybe it wasn't Love at first sight. But it was Love at the first smell of You walking past me. Love at the first touch of that first hug. Love at the first taste of thought that I could make You happy in a life we share—Love at first hearing my name come from Your lips.

TheWayWeShouldHaveBeen

The Way We Should Have Been

Calling someone the one who got away implies that you allowed them to leave without going after them. You were never mine, but I wanted You to be. You are not the one who got away. You are the one that should have always been.

TheWayWeShouldHaveBeen

The Way We Should Have Been

I don't want to be the person I used to be. The person I used to be was quiet when You came around. The person I used to be smiled and acted casually when we talked. The person I used to be never expressed how much You mean to her. The person I used to be would not have told You how beautiful and unique You are. I am no longer that person!

TheWayWeShouldHaveBeen

The Way We Should Have Been

You know me just as I know You. I am the voice in Your mind when You sleep. I am the wind when You step outside and need a jacket. I am the butterflies in Your stomach when You are nervous. I am the heart palpitations when You are afraid. I am the goosebumps on Your body when You are in Love. I am there with You every step of the way, cheering You on in your endeavors. I know You just as You know me because You are with me.

TheWayWeShouldHaveBeen

The Way We Should Have Been

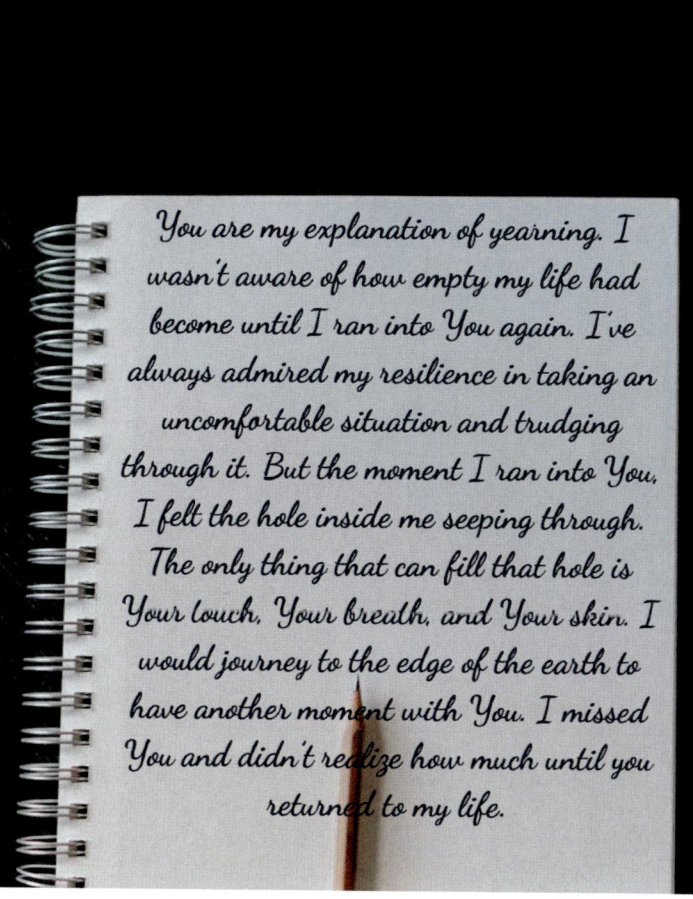

TheWayWeShouldHaveBeen

The Way We Should Have Been

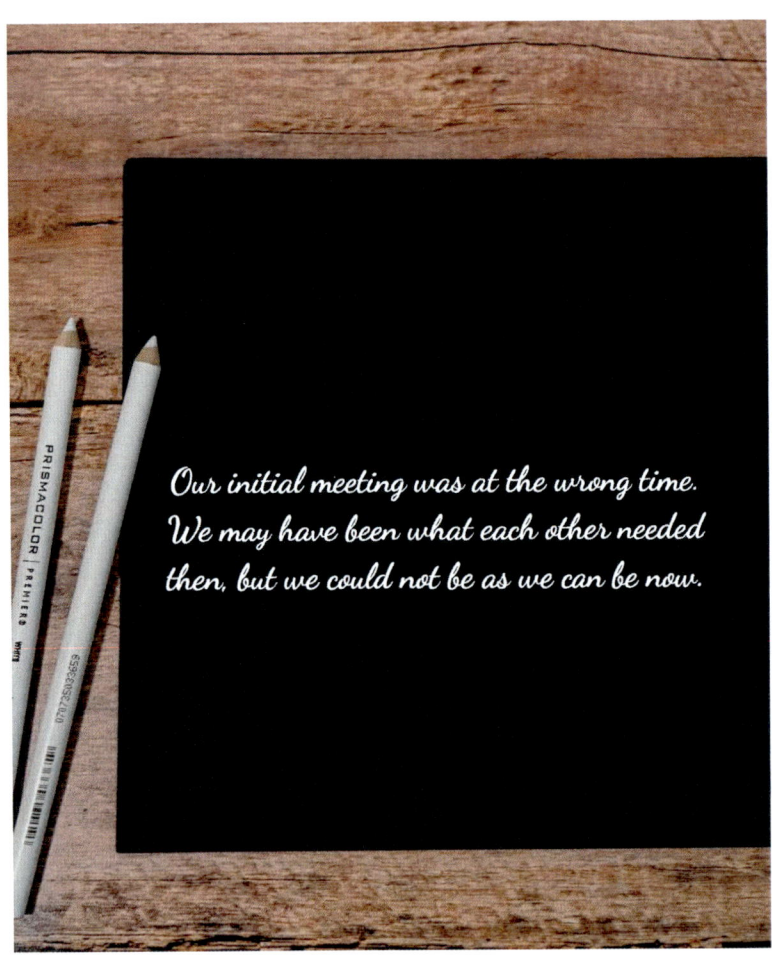

Our initial meeting was at the wrong time. We may have been what each other needed then, but we could not be as we can be now.

TheWayWeShouldHaveBeen

The Way We Should Have Been

I die a little every day that I cannot be with You. I die a little more when I cannot hear Your voice. I die even more so when I cannot reach out to touch You. I'm afraid that when we finally are reunited, there will be a shell of a woman where I once stood.

TheWayWeShouldHaveBeen

The Way We Should Have Been

TheWayWeShouldHaveBeen

The Way We Should Have Been

TheWayWeShouldHaveBeen

The Way We Should Have Been

I want to be there in the presence of Your being. I want to hold on to Your soul's desires. I want Your dreams to become my dreams. I want Your desires to become my desires. My soul craves Your soul.

The Way We Should Have Been

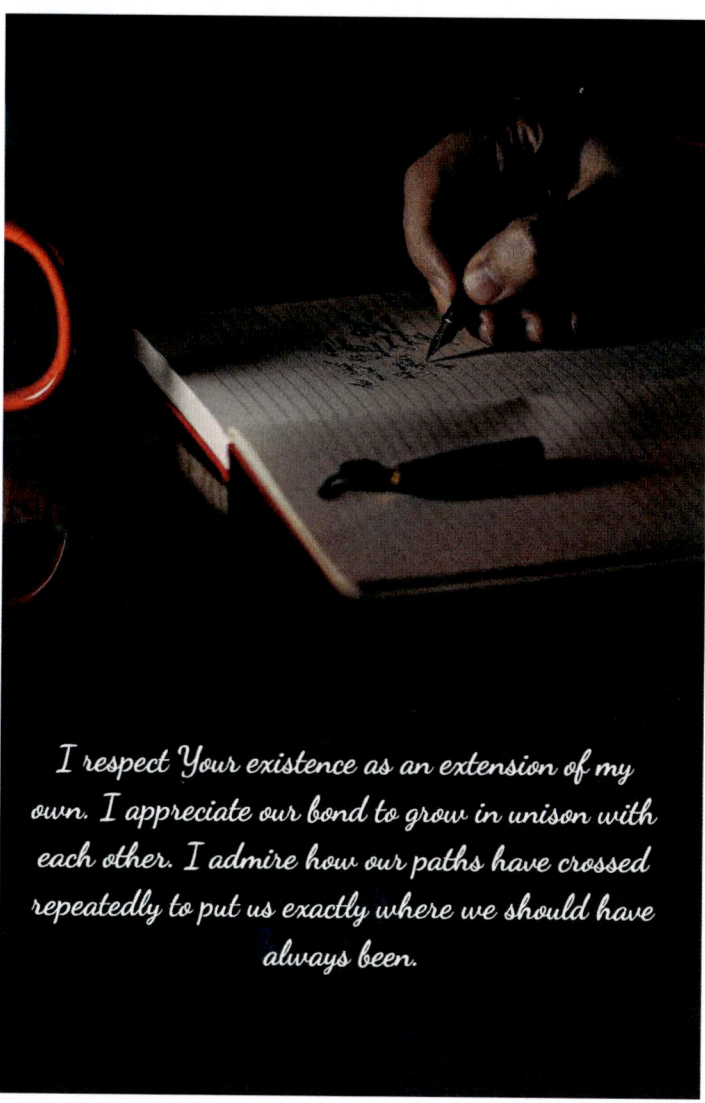

I respect Your existence as an extension of my own. I appreciate our bond to grow in unison with each other. I admire how our paths have crossed repeatedly to put us exactly where we should have always been.

The Way We Should Have Been

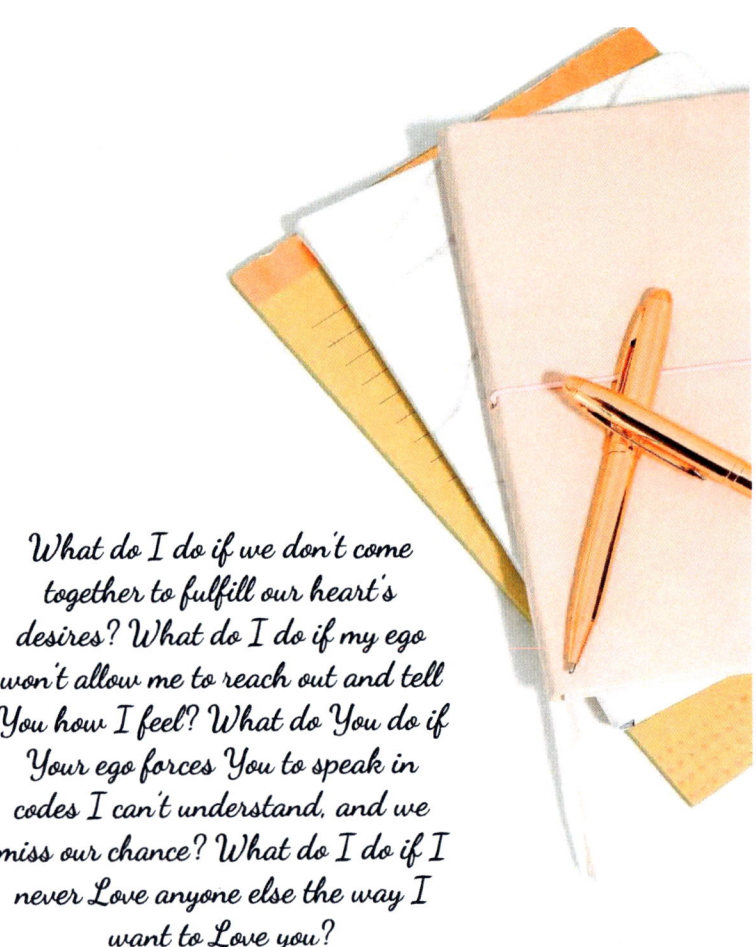

What do I do if we don't come together to fulfill our heart's desires? What do I do if my ego won't allow me to reach out and tell You how I feel? What do You do if Your ego forces You to speak in codes I can't understand, and we miss our chance? What do I do if I never Love anyone else the way I want to Love you?

TheWayWeShouldHaveBeen

The Way We Should Have Been

TheWayWeShouldHaveBeen

The Way We Should Have Been

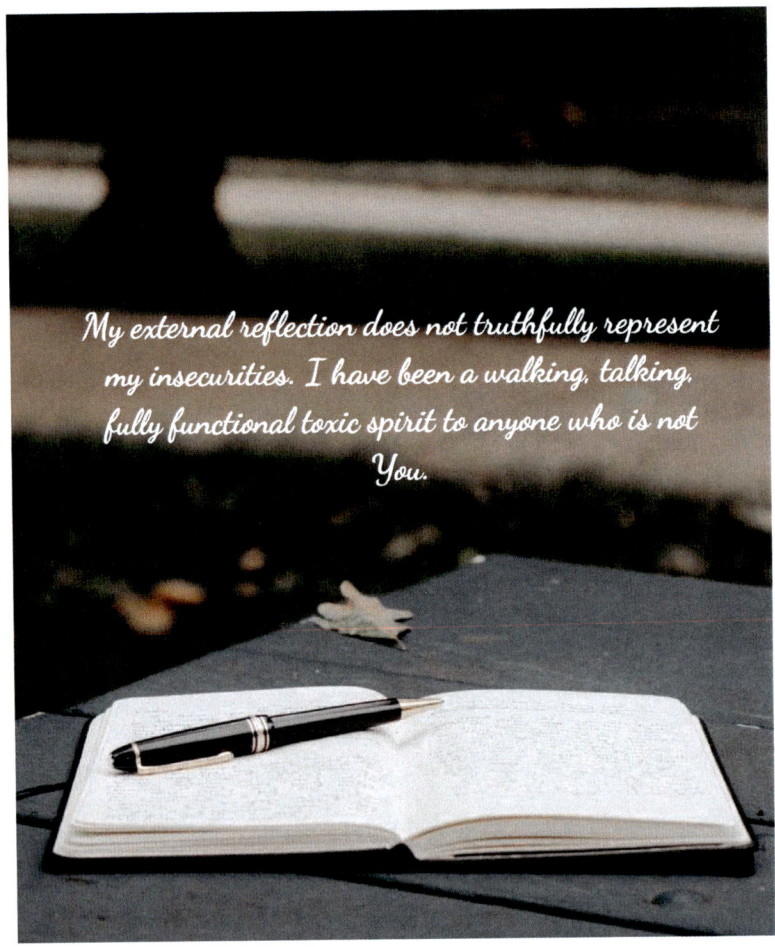

TheWayWeShouldHaveBeen

The Way We Should Have Been

TheWayWeShouldHaveBeen

The Way We Should Have Been

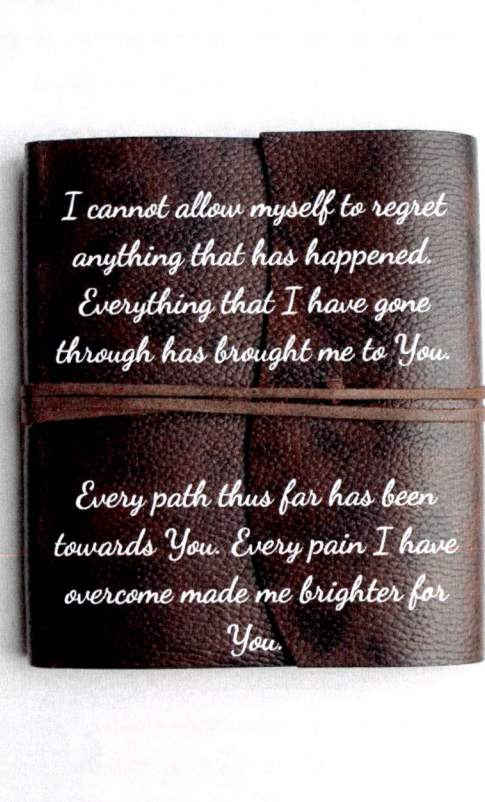

TheWayWeShouldHaveBeen

The Way We Should Have Been

We've never been given a chance. That is why I did not give up and why I will never give up. It may not have been the right time for us, but we can make the time now to finish what we never started.

The Way We Should Have Been

TheWayWeShouldHaveBeen

The Way We Should Have Been

TheWayWeShouldHaveBeen

The Way We Should Have Been

I want to scream for You. I want to shout at the top of my voice, using every fiber of my being and every breath in my body, how much I want You.

TheWayWeShouldHaveBeen

The Way We Should Have Been

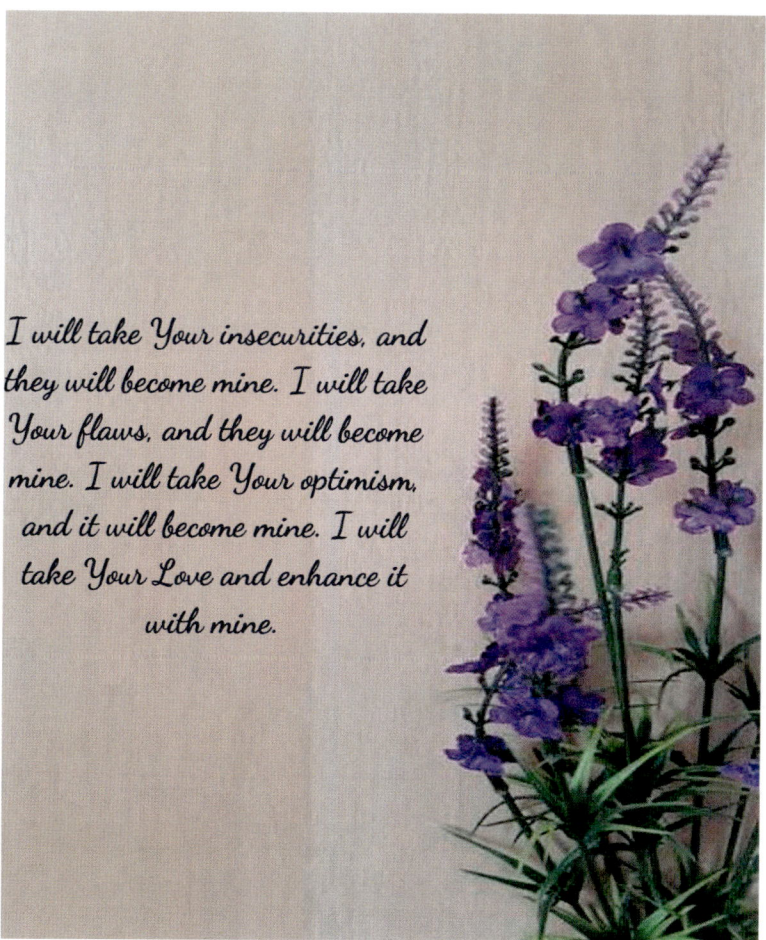

I will take Your insecurities, and they will become mine. I will take Your flaws, and they will become mine. I will take Your optimism, and it will become mine. I will take Your Love and enhance it with mine.

TheWayWeShouldHaveBeen

The Way We Should Have Been

I will speak of this moment in ten years and tell how I almost let my insecurities and ego get the better of me. I will talk of this moment fondly about how I was not afraid to Love and be Loved by You.

TheWayWeShouldHaveBeen

The Way We Should Have Been

TheWayWeShouldHaveBeen

The Way We Should Have Been

TheWayWeShouldHaveBeen

The Way We Should Have Been

When we are together again, we will laugh at the fear that kept us apart. When we are together again, we will rejoice as two souls intertwine. Our auras will emit a beautiful kaleidoscope of colors as our bodies unite in pleasure and desire.

TheWayWeShouldHaveBeen

The Way We Should Have Been

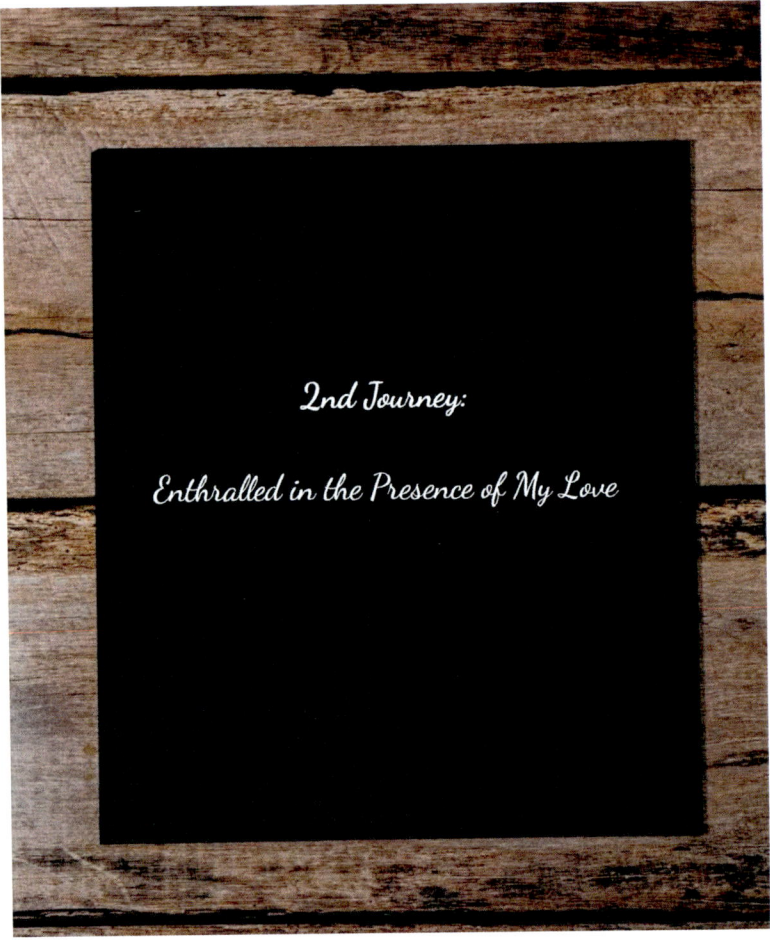

2nd Journey:

Enthralled in the Presence of My Love

TheWayWeShouldHaveBeen

The Way We Should Have Been

TheWayWeShouldHaveBeen

The Way We Should Have Been

TheWayWeShouldHaveBeen

The Way We Should Have Been

> I want to follow You everywhere.
> I want to be wherever You are.

> Even when my Love goes to the bathroom, every second away from You is too long.

TheWayWeShouldHaveBeen

The Way We Should Have Been

No one has ever had this impact on me before. I just wanted to let You know that You have my complete attention. I hang on to Your every word. Your presence invades my thoughts consistently.

The Way We Should Have Been

> One of the worst pains in the world is being in Love with someone who doesn't know it. You can't tell them because of the fear that they won't feel the same. That is true heartache.

TheWayWeShouldHaveBeen

The Way We Should Have Been

I lie in bed at night and talk to You. I Love looking at You and feeling Your breath on my face. You study my face as if You are committing my features to memory. Your fingers outline my lips. Your touch is warm and gentle. Your presence is life renewed.

TheWayWeShouldHaveBeen

The Way We Should Have Been

I didn't know what I needed until You gave it to me. I didn't know what I was lacking until You filled the space. I didn't know what I wanted until You showed up. I didn't know how much I didn't know.

TheWayWeShouldHaveBeen

The Way We Should Have Been

I wrote You letters that You have yet to receive. I whispered thoughts to You that You never heard. I walked next to You, but You have yet to see me. I wrapped my arms around You, but You never felt me.

Can You feel me now?

The Way We Should Have Been

The words escape me sometimes. I am better with pen to paper, regurgitating what my brain failed to release to my lips. My mind overpowers me...., but it also holds me back. I Love how expressive You are. I don't have to wonder what You think or feel because You tell me.

TheWayWeShouldHaveBeen

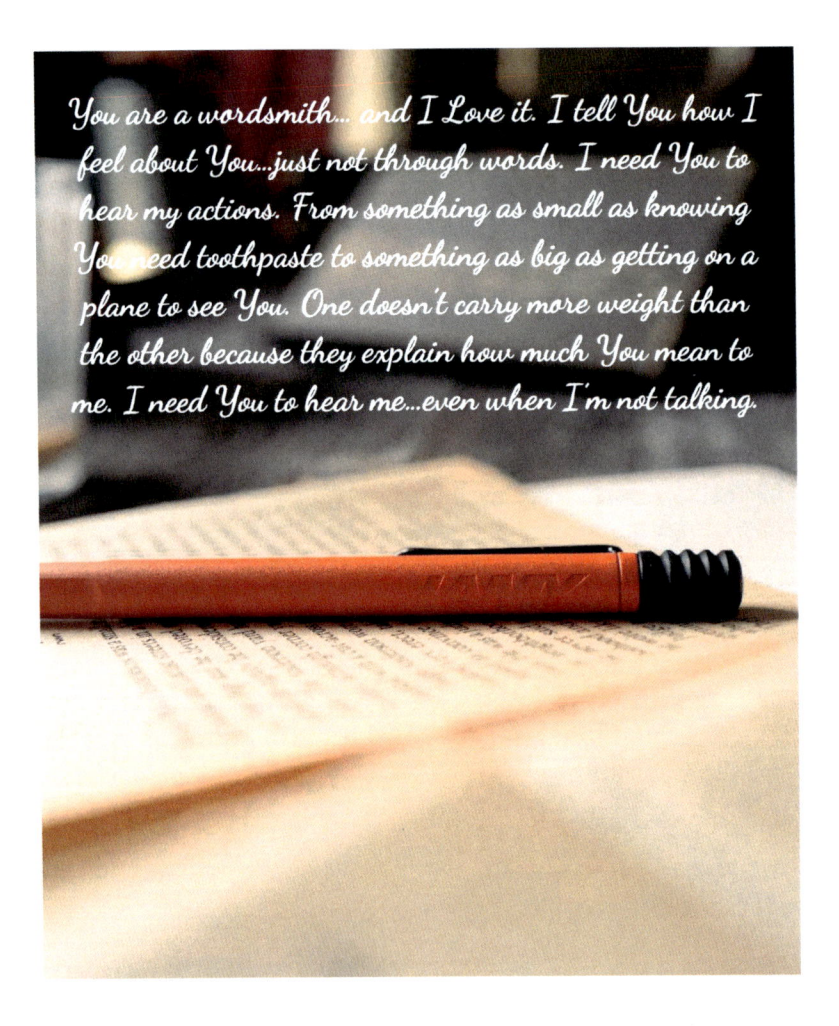

The Way We Should Have Been

You are a wordsmith... and I Love it. I tell You how I feel about You...just not through words. I need You to hear my actions. From something as small as knowing You need toothpaste to something as big as getting on a plane to see You. One doesn't carry more weight than the other because they explain how much You mean to me. I need You to hear me...even when I'm not talking.

TheWayWeShouldHaveBeen

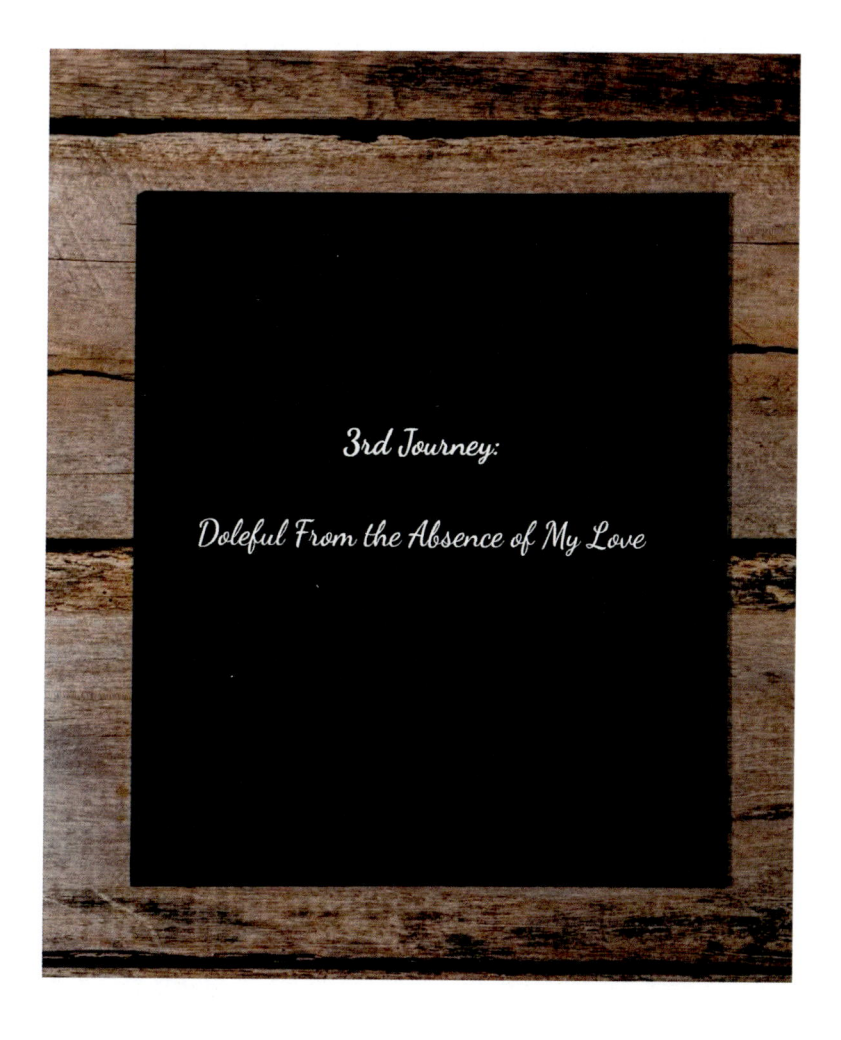

The Way We Should Have Been

3rd Journey:

Doleful From the Absence of My Love

TheWayWeShouldHaveBeen

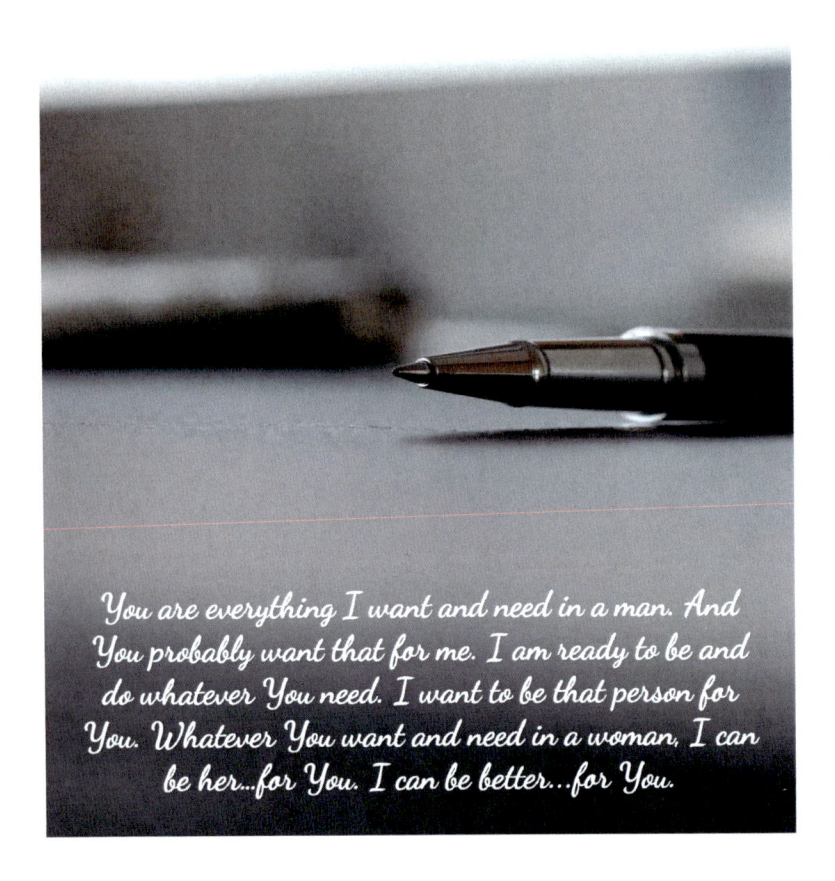

The Way We Should Have Been

You are everything I want and need in a man. And You probably want that for me. I am ready to be and do whatever You need. I want to be that person for You. Whatever You want and need in a woman, I can be her...for You. I can be better...for You.

TheWayWeShouldHaveBeen

The Way We Should Have Been

I wanted it to be You so bad that I wouldn't even entertain the idea that You didn't want it to be me.

TheWayWeShouldHaveBeen

The Way We Should Have Been

I know my life's purpose, and You are a part of that purpose. Please do not fight me on this. You won't scare me away. I see You and still want You.

TheWayWeShouldHaveBeen

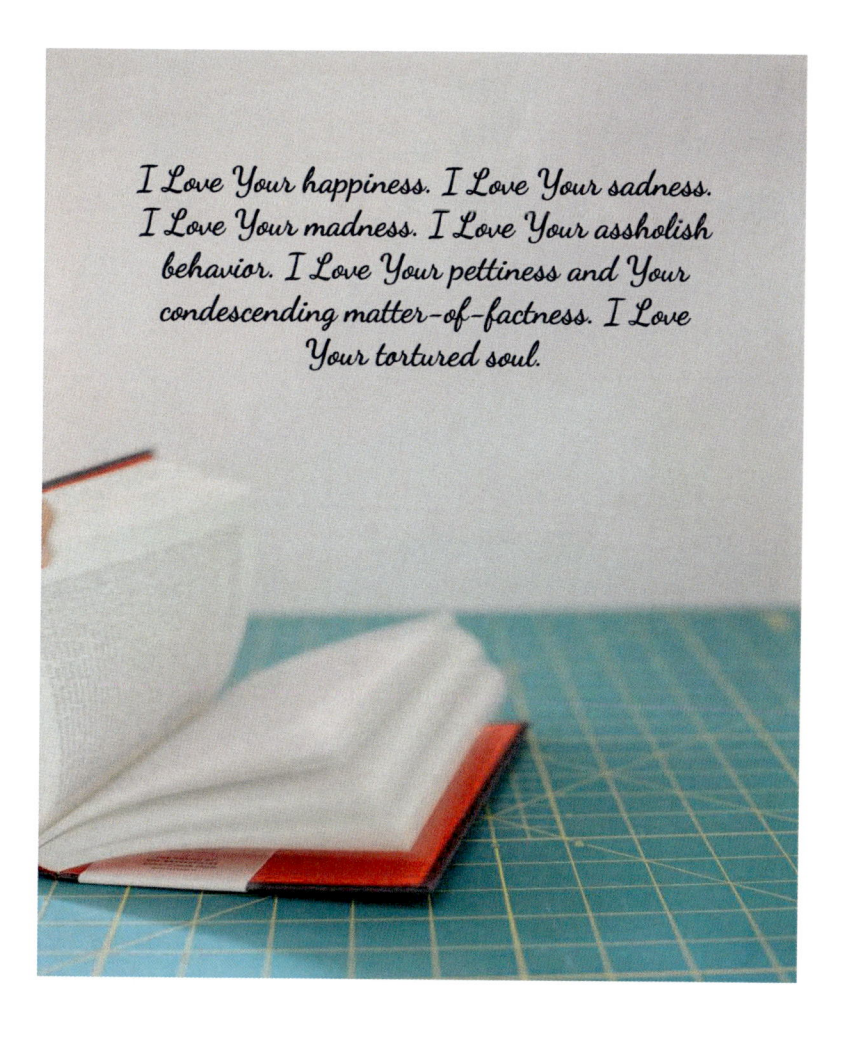

The Way We Should Have Been

I Love Your happiness. I Love Your sadness. I Love Your madness. I Love Your assholish behavior. I Love Your pettiness and Your condescending matter-of-factness. I Love Your tortured soul.

TheWayWeShouldHaveBeen

The Way We Should Have Been

> I Love listening to You and thinking, "That shit doesn't make a lick of sense, but I Love how His mind works."

TheWayWeShouldHaveBeen

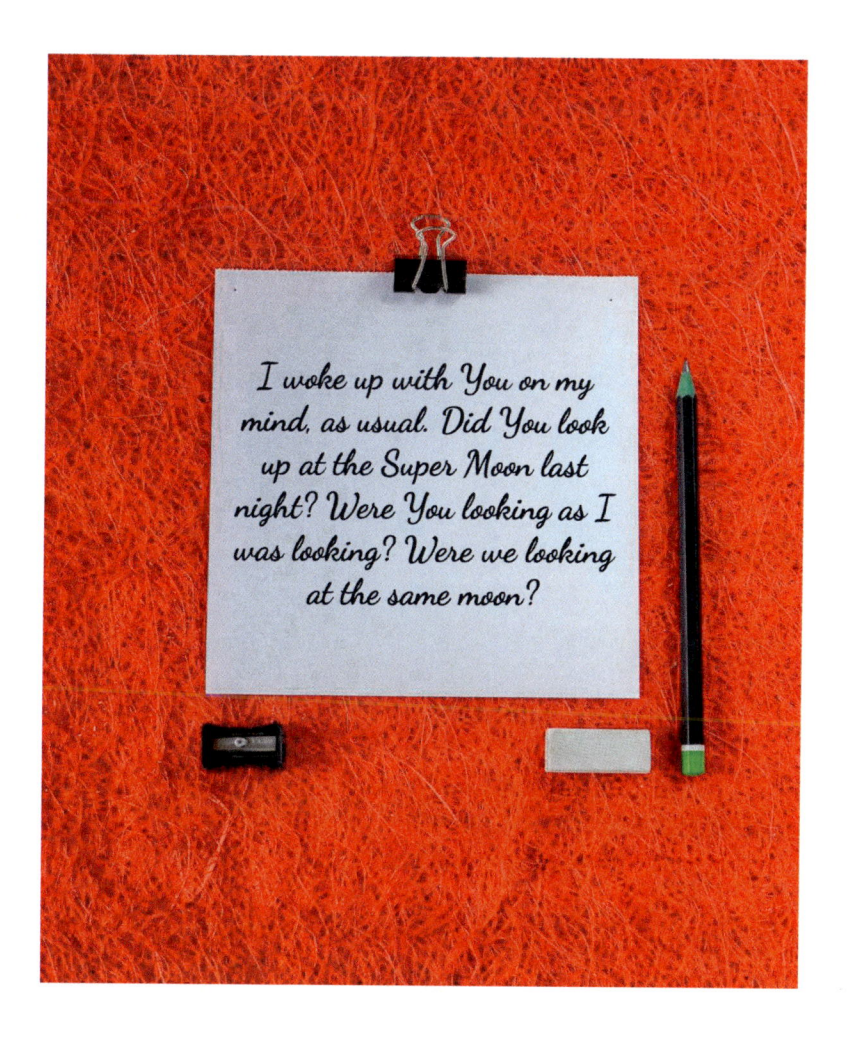

The Way We Should Have Been

I woke up with You on my mind, as usual. Did You look up at the Super Moon last night? Were You looking as I was looking? Were we looking at the same moon?

TheWayWeShouldHaveBeen

The Way We Should Have Been

I know You can feel me. Tell me. Please tell me how You feel. What are You afraid of? Feel my thoughts. Hear my wishes. See my love...See, My Love.

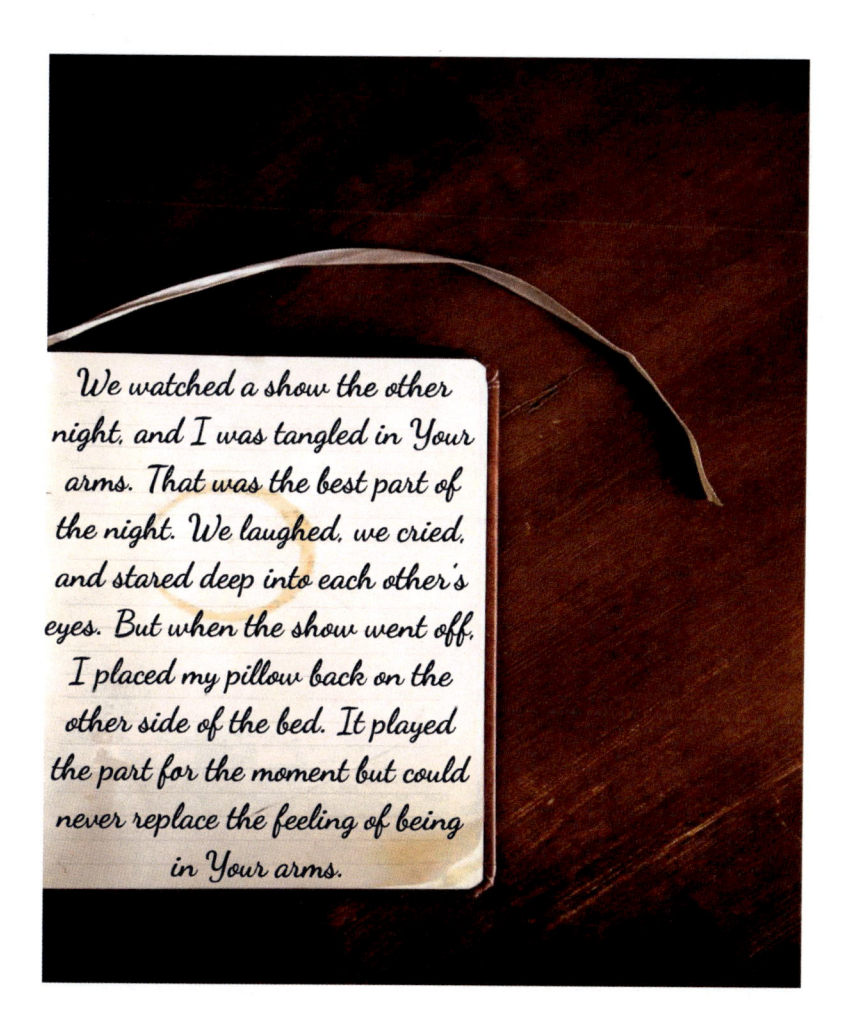

The Way We Should Have Been

> We watched a show the other night, and I was tangled in Your arms. That was the best part of the night. We laughed, we cried, and stared deep into each other's eyes. But when the show went off, I placed my pillow back on the other side of the bed. It played the part for the moment but could never replace the feeling of being in Your arms.

TheWayWeShouldHaveBeen

The Way We Should Have Been

Do You cry for me? Do You scream for our Love? Do You yell at the thought of me not being in Your arms? Am I staring back at You when you lay Your beautiful head on Your pillow at night? Can You feel me?

I can feel You.

The Way We Should Have Been

I am a pleaser. You are a healer. You heal the insecurities in me. You heal the doubts in me. You heal the pains and regrets in me. Ego and Pride aside: in Your arms, my body is revitalized. Let me please You.

TheWayWeShouldHaveBeen

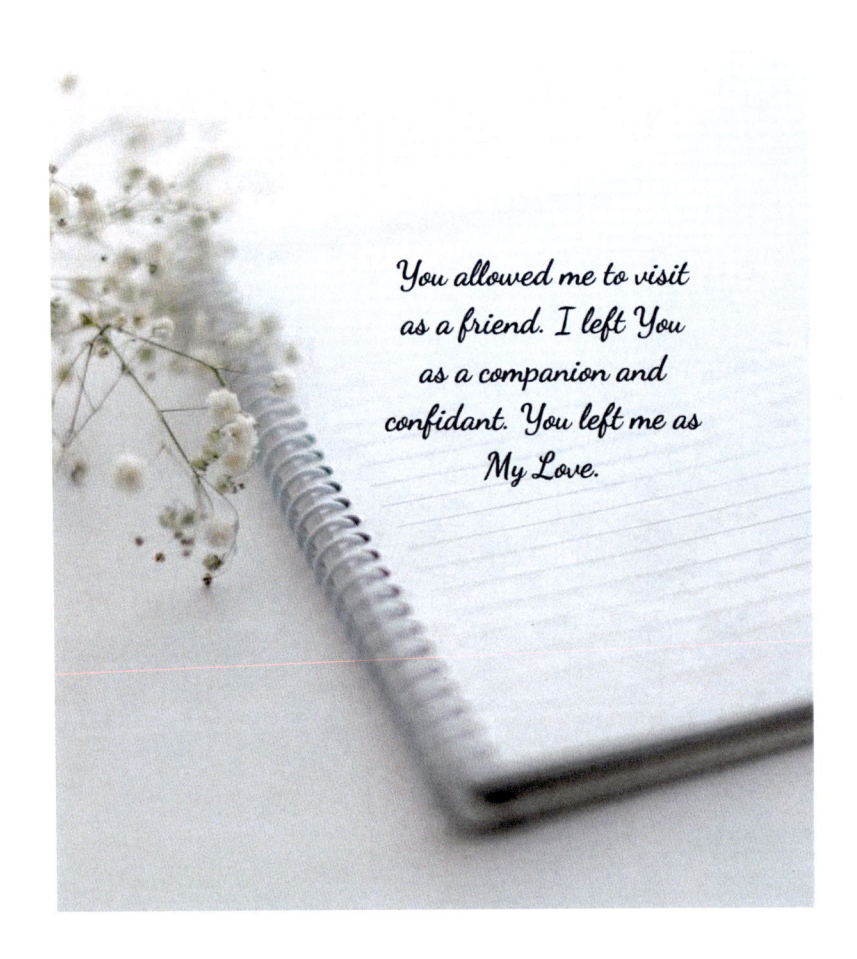

The Way We Should Have Been

> You allowed me to visit as a friend. I left You as a companion and confidant. You left me as My Love.

TheWayWeShouldHaveBeen

The Way We Should Have Been

I shared a weak moment with You to be transparent. I don't think it was received how I envisioned. I'm going to try to be more cognizant next time. I can do better. I can be better...for You.

TheWayWeShouldHaveBeen

The Way We Should Have Been

I've purchased a ring to wear on my ring finger. I wanted to let everyone know that I was taken. You are not claiming me anymore, but I am claiming You. I'm trying to be patient because You may need time to realize that you want to be with me.

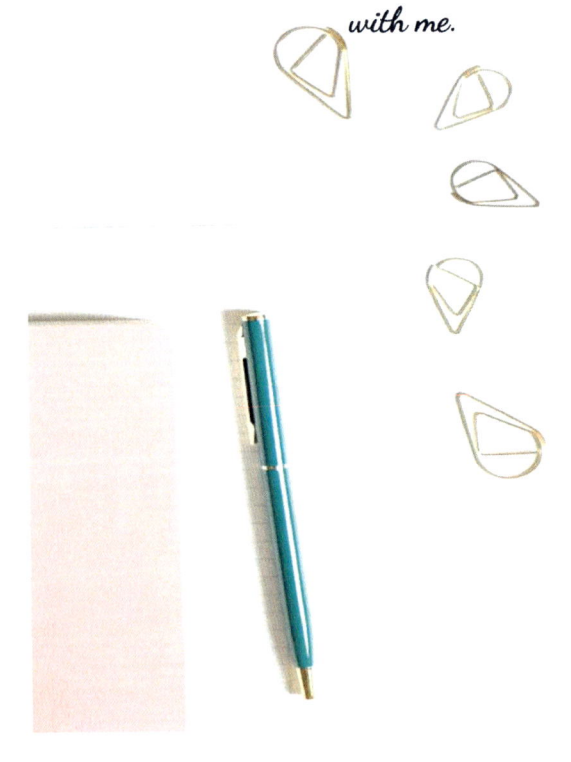

TheWayWeShouldHaveBeen

The Way We Should Have Been

Let me show You how I can love You. Let me show You how beautiful You are. Let me show You how I adore every thought, every whisper, every tear, every spoken word, every glance, every touch, every laugh, every snore, every kiss, every moan, every silent breath, every phone call, every text message, and every single inch of Your body.

Let me.

TheWayWeShouldHaveBeen

The Way We Should Have Been

We have so little time on this Earth.. I don't want to spend another second, another minute, another hour, another day without You.

TheWayWeShouldHaveBeen

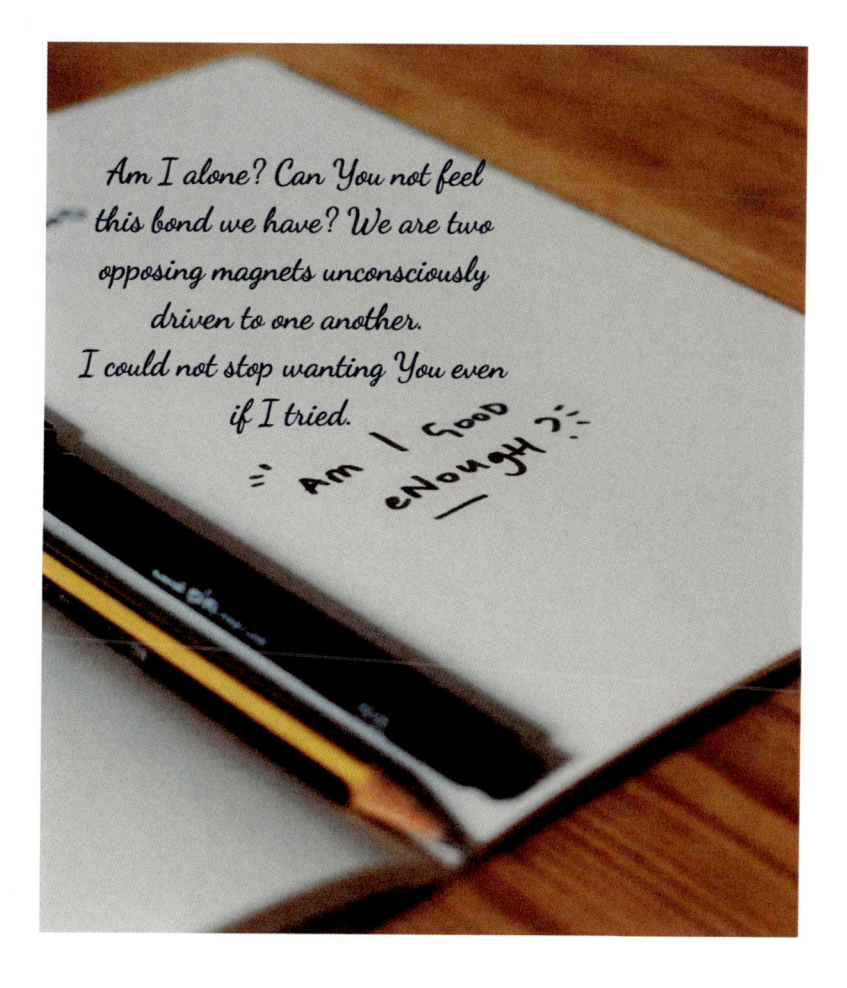

The Way We Should Have Been

Am I alone? Can You not feel this bond we have? We are two opposing magnets unconsciously driven to one another.
I could not stop wanting You even if I tried.

:' Am I Good eNoughH ?:'

TheWayWeShouldHaveBeen

The Way We Should Have Been

I've seen behind the curtain. I've witnessed the secrets of the magic trick. I cannot pretend I don't know what it means to Love You. I cannot pretend You aren't my every waking thought. I cannot pretend I do not want to lie in Your arms, feel Your warmth, smell Your scent, or touch Your skin. I cannot pretend.

TheWayWeShouldHaveBeen

The Way We Should Have Been

I walked in desire with You. I bathed in ecstasy with You. I hiked mountains of pleasure with You. I tasted happiness with You. I ran marathons of stimulations with You. I smelled life renewed with You. I saw my future with You.

TheWayWeShouldHaveBeen

The Way We Should Have Been

When I look at other men, I see only You. When they kiss my lips, I taste only You. When they touch my skin, I feel only You. When they speak to me, I hear only You.

TheWayWeShouldHaveBeen

The Way We Should Have Been

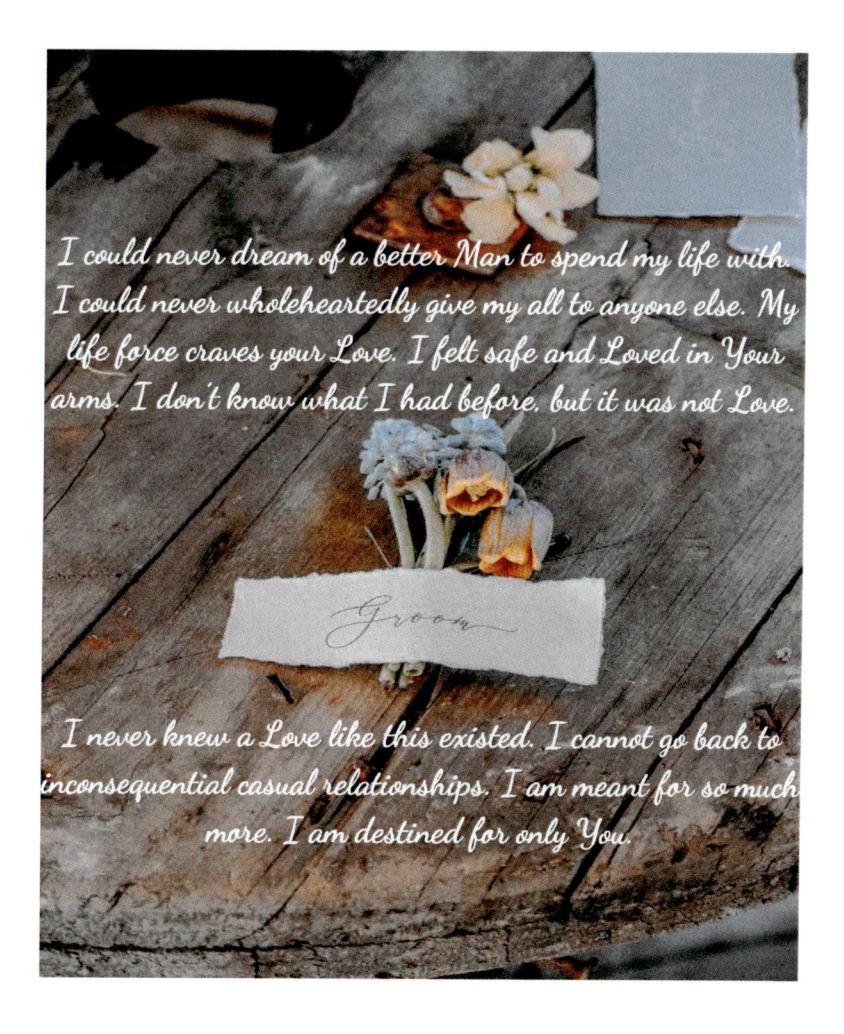

I could never dream of a better Man to spend my life with. I could never wholeheartedly give my all to anyone else. My life force craves your Love. I felt safe and Loved in Your arms. I don't know what I had before, but it was not Love.

Groom

I never knew a Love like this existed. I cannot go back to inconsequential casual relationships. I am meant for so much more. I am destined for only You.

TheWayWeShouldHaveBeen

The Way We Should Have Been

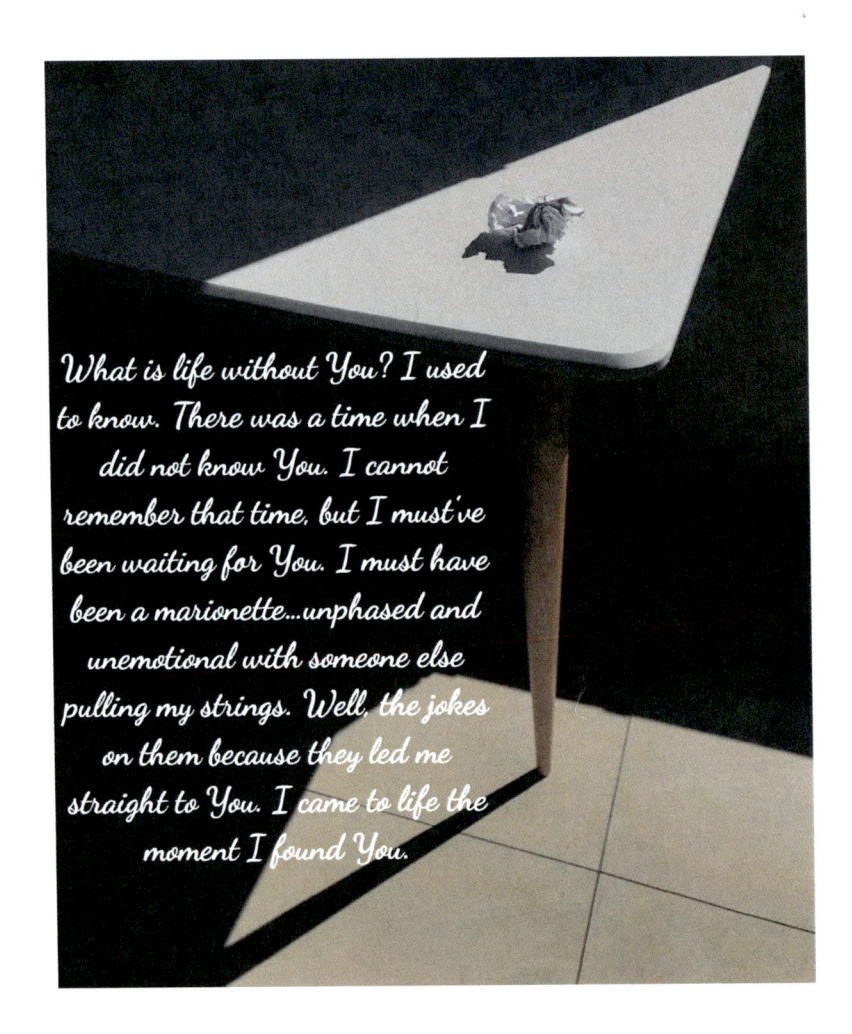

What is life without You? I used to know. There was a time when I did not know You. I cannot remember that time, but I must've been waiting for You. I must have been a marionette...unphased and unemotional with someone else pulling my strings. Well, the jokes on them because they led me straight to You. I came to life the moment I found You.

TheWayWeShouldHaveBeen

The Way We Should Have Been

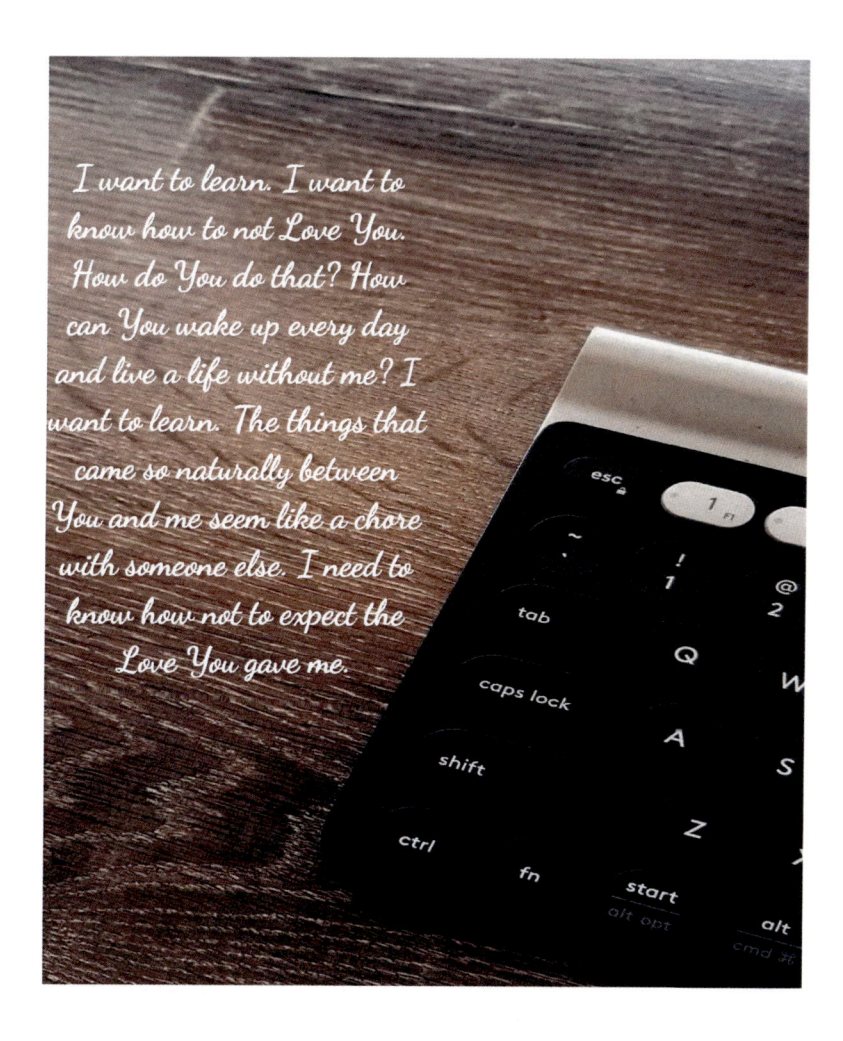

I want to learn. I want to know how to not Love You. How do You do that? How can You wake up every day and live a life without me? I want to learn. The things that came so naturally between You and me seem like a chore with someone else. I need to know how not to expect the Love You gave me.

TheWayWeShouldHaveBeen

The Way We Should Have Been

> We promised each other that we would not have to settle anymore. We promised each other forever. Forever is shorter than I imagined it to be. I am forced to settle for less than what I deserve. I am forced to settle for less than You.

TheWayWeShouldHaveBeen

The Way We Should Have Been

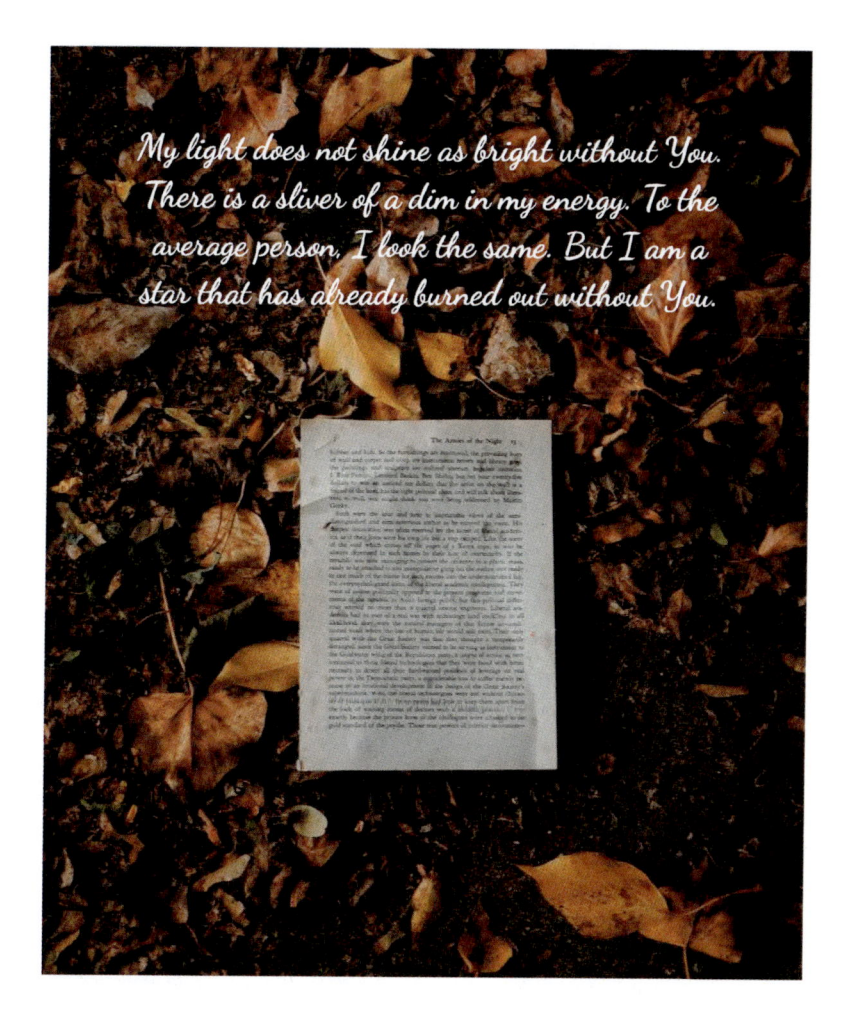

My light does not shine as bright without You. There is a sliver of a dim in my energy. To the average person, I look the same. But I am a star that has already burned out without You.

TheWayWeShouldHaveBeen

The Way We Should Have Been

Please show me. Show me how to Love You. If I fall short of giving You what You need, show me. Don't just take Your Love away and abandon me. Show me how I can make it right. Please show me. Show me the path back to Your heart. It's too dark out here, and I can't find my way. Please show me.

TheWayWeShouldHaveBeen

The Way We Should Have Been

Let's start over. Nothing is set in stone. We can choose to be better to each other going forward. We can choose to be better for each other going forward. We can make that promise to each other going forward. We can be...together... going forward.

TheWayWeShouldHaveBeen

The Way We Should Have Been

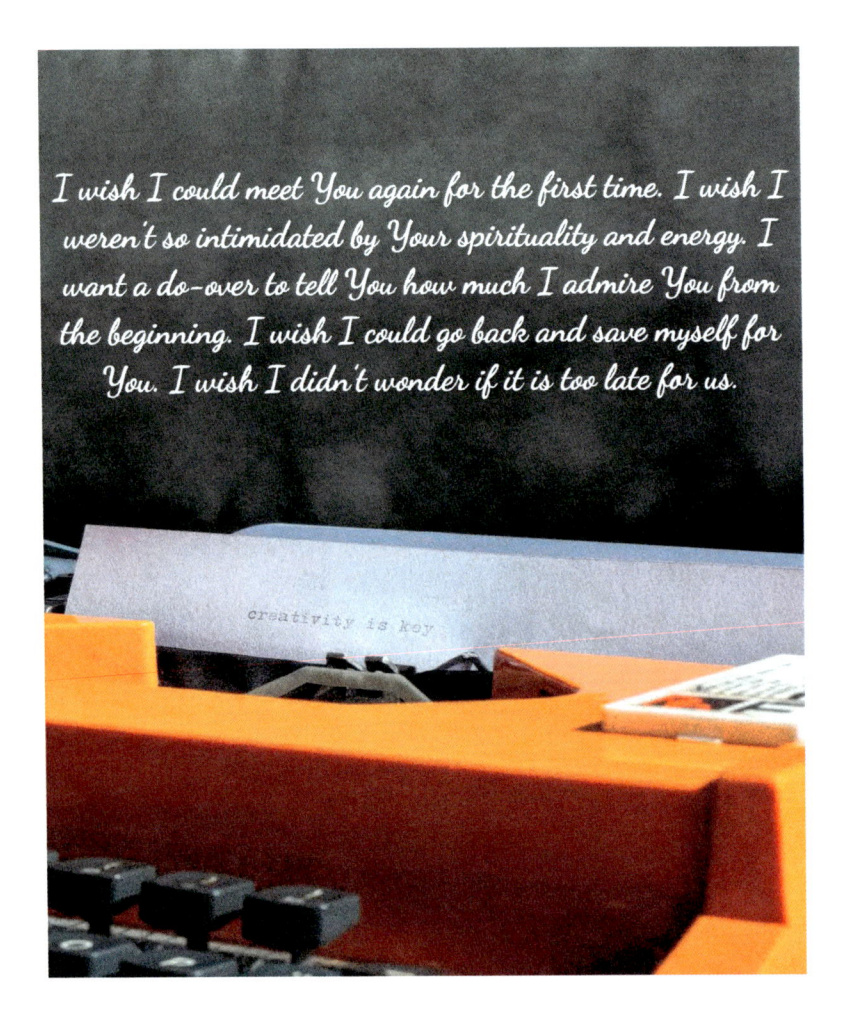

I wish I could meet You again for the first time. I wish I weren't so intimidated by Your spirituality and energy. I want a do-over to tell You how much I admire You from the beginning. I wish I could go back and save myself for You. I wish I didn't wonder if it is too late for us.

creativity is key

TheWayWeShouldHaveBeen

The Way We Should Have Been

It's a lonely highway out here without You. This is the longest journey I've had to take without You. I don't want to take this road trip without You.

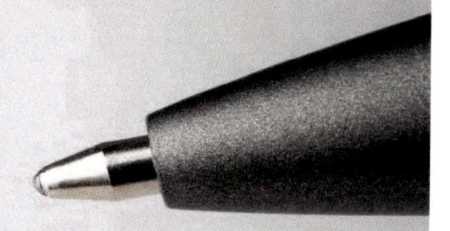

Success isn't as sweet without You to share it with. Obstacles seem more daunting without Your support. Life is life-ing more without Your presence.

TheWayWeShouldHaveBeen

The Way We Should Have Been

My sun and my moon orbit your eternal flame. The fire in Your eyes is only matched by the air You breathe. Since fire needs air to live, Your life force is everlasting. It draws me in and captures me with promises of desire. Your burning embrace stuns my senses and highlights my energy. I can be my full potential with You by my side.

TheWayWeShouldHaveBeen

The Way We Should Have Been

I will wait for You. You are worth my time. You are worth my thoughts. You are worth my feelings. You are worth waiting for. I will patiently wait for You.

TheWayWeShouldHaveBeen

The Way We Should Have Been

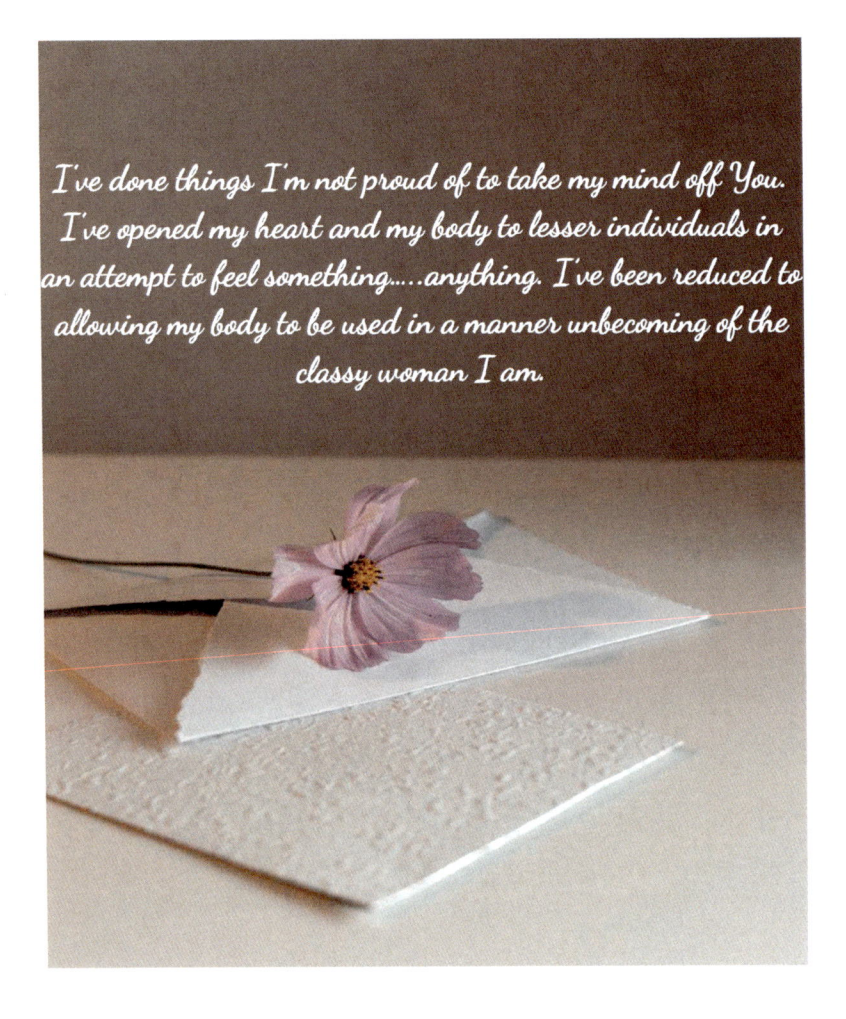

I've done things I'm not proud of to take my mind off You. I've opened my heart and my body to lesser individuals in an attempt to feel something......anything. I've been reduced to allowing my body to be used in a manner unbecoming of the classy woman I am.

TheWayWeShouldHaveBeen

The Way We Should Have Been

I can draw Your face from memory. I have studied Your features and burned them permanently into my mind. I know every laugh line, wrinkle, worry, anger, concentrating, focus, hungry, sentimental, horny, indifferent, thoughtful expression. I want them all.

TheWayWeShouldHaveBeen

The Way We Should Have Been

Look
Look to feel, not to see.
Look at my actions, not my words.
Look at how I respond to your words.
Look at how I react to your actions.
Do not see me. Feel me.
Feel my love.
Feel, My Love…

TheWayWeShouldHaveBeen

The Way We Should Have Been

Can you feel me now...

TheWayWeShouldHaveBeen

The Way We Should Have Been

Afterthought

Why would You do that? Why would You come into my secure vault...my locked, comfortable, happy place to show me what I can never have? I was blissful in my ignorance. I only knew what I was missing because You picked the lock and announced Your presence. I can never go back to the dark. The door is open, and I've stepped into the Sun.

Why would You do that? The dark was my friend. I could see it. I could smell it. I could touch and taste it. It brought me comfort. It was safe. The Sun is full of desire. I want it, but I cannot look upon it. It is out of reach. I cannot taste or smell it. It is a pleasurable craving that I can feel but can't fully experience.

It makes my dark seem insignificant in comparison. It teases me with promises of pleasure and an erotic sense of pain if I were to get too close. I want that pain. I like that pleasure. I need to feel engulfed by its heated intimacy. My body yearns for that burning embrace.

This longing is not natural. I can never have it. The dark is absolute. The dark is safe and calls out to me. The Sun is a dream I do not want to wake up from.

Why would You do that?

TheWayWeShouldHaveBeen

Made in the USA
Middletown, DE
22 December 2023